# THE ENEMY

## A Story From World War II

*Look out for other titles in the Survivors series:*

SURVIVORS

# THE
# ENEMY

*A Story From World War II*

James Riordan

HODDER
Wayland

*an imprint of Hodder Children's Books*

Book editor: Katie Orchard
Map illustrator: Peter Bull

Published in Great Britain in 2001 by Hodder Wayland
An imprint of Hodder Children's Books Limited

British Library Cataloguing in Publication Data

Riordan, James 1936–
  The Enemy: A Story From World War II. – (Survivors)
  1. World War, 1939–1945 – Social aspects – Juvenile fiction
  2. Children's stories
  I. Title
  823.9'14 [J]

ISBN 0 7502 3439 3

Typeset by Avon Dataset Ltd, Bidford-on-Avon, Warks
www.avondataset.com

Printed and bound in Great Britain by
Clays Ltd, St Ives plc

# Introduction

When the German leader Adolf Hitler invaded Poland in early September 1939, France and Britain declared war on Germany. World War II had begun. During that autumn and winter British soldiers started arriving in northern France to join French and Belgian troops – in case the Germans attacked. But nothing happened!

It was a strange time: the British called it the 'phoney war', the Germans simply *Sitzkrieg* – the sit-down war. Everything changed one Whitsun weekend that altered the course of history. The Germans launched their *Blitzkrieg* on 10 May 1940 and, in three weeks, pushed the Allies back to the coast. By 24 May, only Dunkirk was holding out. As many as 350,000 soldiers were trapped there, with only the sea at their backs.

Then began the 'Miracle of Dunkirk'. Almost 1,000 boats crossed the Channel to take soldiers to safety in England – destroyers and paddle steamers, ferry boats and fishing smacks – every size and shape of boat. 'Operation Dynamo' started on Sunday 26 May and ended a week later. It saved the lives of some 200,000 men. The rest died in battle or were taken prisoner.

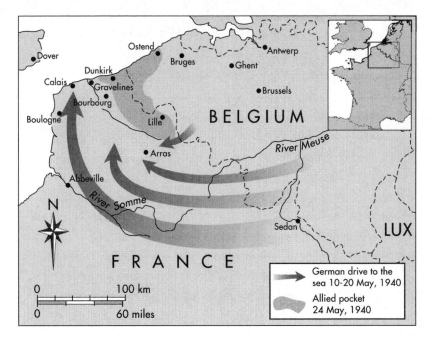

This map shows the sweep of the German tanks, forcing the Allies to the coast, resulting in the Allied pocket – the last part of free France – at Dunkirk on 24 May 1940.

For Nadine and Sean

*One*

# Remembering

As far as the eye could see, there were row upon row of gravestones. But that wasn't all. The grass was cut, the stones gleamed white and clean in the sunshine and the whole place was as neat and tidy as a country garden.

The sign above the arched entrance said: *BRITISH WAR CEMETERY.*

Anne-Marie and Marcel were staying with their grandmother for a few days in the village of Gravelines, just a few kilometres from Dunkirk.

While Gran unpacked a picnic lunch in the shade of an oak tree, Anne-Marie and Marcel walked slowly down an aisle between graves, reading the words inscribed on the tombstones out loud. Many were difficult to understand:

*Pte. John Walker, aged 19. Royal Sussex, died*
*24 May 1940*

*Gunner Alfred Baldwin, aged 18. 1ˢᵗ Cameronians,*
*died 26 May 1940*
*Major D. F. Callandar, aged 32. East Surreys,*
*died 26 May 1940*
*Corp. George Andrew, aged 24. 4ᵗʰ Royal Tank Regiment,*
*died 28 May 1940*

And so the list went on.

When they returned to sit down on the grass verge with Gran, Anne-Marie and Marcel were oddly silent. Even when they talked, they did so in whispers, as in church.

'So many,' murmured Anne-Marie.

'Did you know anyone who died in the war, Gran?' asked Marcel.

For a few moments the grey-haired woman was silent, her green eyes gazing across the gravestones. Then she spoke, as if to the dead themselves, 'Yes. Oh, yes . . . I certainly did.'

Later that afternoon, Anne-Marie and Marcel were sitting together on a rose-patterned sofa by the window of Gran's cottage. When Gran disappeared into the little kitchen, they glanced about the room. The once-cream wallpaper was now brown and cracked, covered here and there with old prints of soldiers on horses and splendid castles. Upon the side-table next to them were several framed black-and-white photographs. One image that caught Anne-Marie's eye was of a little girl about her own age. The girl had two long plaits and a freckled face. She was grinning awkwardly, as if unused to having her picture taken. She was carrying a milk pail in each hand.

Towards the back of the table, Anne-Marie saw the same girl standing between two young men. The men seemed to be invalids, one in uniform, sitting in wicker chairs and smiling shyly.

When Gran entered, Anne-Marie turned her gaze away, guiltily, as if she'd wandered into a bedroom uninvited. Gran put down a tray on the low table before the two children.

'This is my own plum jam,' she said proudly, pouring their bowls of hot chocolate. 'Dig in while I tell you my story. When I've finished, I'll show you something interesting.'

Picking up the first picture that Anne-Marie had noticed, she murmured, half to herself, 'That's me when I was twelve, at the outbreak of war. Ah, what a little scamp I was then. Thankfully, the photo doesn't show my shame: bright ginger hair – "Hair to light a fire with," as Papa used to say. Maman wasn't so kind: "Ginger brings bad luck," was her comment. I think she blamed the war on my hair! We had a farm then. It was my job to feed

3

the chickens, collect up the eggs and milk the cows. Well, the war put a stop to most of our farming. Papa and my brother Gérard went off to do their duty. Like all women and girls in those days, Maman and I did what we could to keep the farm going. The animals still had to be looked after; it wasn't their fault there was a war on . . .'

*Two*

# Billy

I remember English soldiers marching over the cobblestones as if it were yesterday. After them rumbled the tanks – 'Matildas', they called them. We lined the road, tossing flowers on to lorries and tanks. Some of the older, bolder girls ran into the road, hugging and kissing the young Tommies, our name for all English soldiers. They looked so young and brave and handsome. Boys and old men gave them presents – beer, cigarettes, freshly baked rolls. They were awfully skinny and hungry-looking.

We were ever so happy to see the English soldiers. They and our own boys made us feel safe. No enemy would get past them! How wrong we were . . .

For a few weeks the English soldiers camped in our meadow among the molehills and cow pats. Mind you, they were always moaning about the awful food and the rain . . . That autumn it rained cats and dogs. The poor

Tommies complained about their leaky tents, their wet clothes and blankets. They had to sleep on the grass with just a groundsheet beneath them.

It wasn't long before the lads were bored stiff, waiting for some action. But the Germans were elsewhere, killing Poles, Danes and Norwegians. Many of us thought they didn't have the guts to turn on France and England. Or perhaps they were leaving us till last?

Most days RAF planes would roar overhead and we'd run out of school to wave to them. They were on their way to Germany to drop leaflets, telling people what a nasty, wicked man Adolf Hitler was.

You see, through the autumn of 1939 and spring of 1940, we didn't see any bombs or fighting. It was all quiet on the western front. In a way the war was good fun for us kids. We used to look up at the big sausage gas bags with elephant ears flying over the nearby airfield. Those barrage balloons were supposed to scare off enemy planes. But none came! No Stukas, Messerschmitts or Heinkels. We'd never even heard such names then; but it wouldn't be long before we knew each one just by their drone or whine.

Not that life was all fun and games. There were always rumours flying about: 'The Germans are coming!' or, 'They're due at dawn!' That sort of thing. The longer the lull lasted, the more the soldiers were on edge. We were *all* getting nervy. Maman and I worried about Papa and my brother Gérard, who were with the French troops, guarding our frontier defences. We used to get letters sent from Sedan on the River Meuse; and we read and re-read them till they fell apart like dry autumn leaves.

Some of the English officers didn't trust us – even though we were supposed to be allies. They did what they could to stop their men from making friends with us. One day, an officer barged into our cottage with a big, beefy sergeant major. The officer carried a stick under his arm, rather like a headmaster come to cane us. He was coldly polite, but unfriendly, frowning and pointing his stick at Maman. After questioning her about Papa, he asked whether we'd ever been to Germany or if we spoke German. Silly man!

Finally, he got to the point. 'Why is your washing on the line?'

'I beg your pardon?' asked Maman.

The officer coughed, then said, blushing, 'I mean, why are your knickers next to a sheet and a blouse?'

We just stared at him, open-mouthed. Was he off his head or was his French really bad? What on earth was he talking about? All of a sudden, it became clear.

'We think your clothes-line is a semaphore message to the Germans,' he said.

At that, Maman couldn't help herself. She burst out laughing. That made the officer even redder. He gave an order to the sergeant major who snapped to attention and saluted. 'Yes, sir. Right away, sir!'

Next thing we knew, he was turning everything upside down, searching for something.

'What are you looking for?' asked Maman.

'Your transmitter.'

'What?'

'For contacting the enemy.'

After half an hour, the sergeant major appeared, having searched the house, barn, cow shed and hen house. Bits of straw still stuck to his khaki uniform and he smelled sourly of chicken droppings.

'Any luck, sergeant major?' asked the officer sternly.

'I've found this, sir.' He held up a torch with a look of triumph on his shiny face.

It took us another half an hour to explain that, no, we didn't shine the torch at night for enemy aircraft – we'd seen none anyway. Nor did we plough give-away patterns in our cornfield to guide German pilots. As he could see, we hadn't ploughed the field at all.

Finally, the two men left, taking our torch with them.

We weren't the only ones to attract the eagle-eye of the intelligence officers. They were convinced that spies were everywhere. Once they even searched a group of nuns. Presumably, they thought the nuns could be German soldiers disguised in black habits and white starched hats.

The sergeant paid particular attention to hands, feet and chins before declaring loudly to the company commander, 'All present and correct, *sah!* All women, no men, *sah!*'

'Carry on, ladies,' was all the commanding officer said.

Despite this, the villagers generally got on well with the Tommies. Now and then there'd be a concert party for the troops followed by a dance in the church hall. Once a famous English film star, Gracie Fields, came over and sang for the lads. Maman wouldn't allow me to go to the dances. At twelve I was too young, she said. But I did make friends with one English soldier.

I was coming back from milking late one afternoon in March, when I bumped into a young soldier in the lane.

'May I help you carry your pail, love?' he said.

I couldn't speak much English and he obviously didn't speak any French. But he had a kind and friendly face; and he made signs towards my milk pails, so I understood what he was saying.

We *were* supposed to be allies, so I said, 'Thank you, sir. That's very kind of you.'

9

He carried my milk pails all the way home. At the door Maman invited him in for a bowl of fresh milk. She spoke some English, so we managed to get on OK – just about. He told us his name was Billy, and that he was a regular in the army. To our surprise he said he'd come to France straight from Buckingham Palace – where he was in the Guards, looking after King George, Queen Mary and their little daughters Elizabeth and Margaret.

After that he came to see us regularly, showing us photos of himself in uniform at the palace. Very smart and handsome he looked, too. He also brought pictures of his family: his mum, dad and brothers.

Billy did some jobs for us round the farm – fixing the tractor, putting slates on the roof, nailing some planks to the barn wall. In exchange, Maman fed him and taught him some French; and he gave me English lessons. I picked it up quite quickly, as I'd already done a year of English at school. But it's different hearing it, as he said, 'from the horse's mouth', isn't it? He used to call me Marie or Little Gingernob, and I called him Billy-Tommy.

A couple of months later, in early May, Billy's regiment was moved to Arras, half-way to Paris. And I thought that was that – I'd never see him again.

Little did I know the adventures – and the tragedy – to come.

10

*Three*

# The Germans Attack

After Billy's departure, life in Gravelines went on much as before, although no more Tommies passed through the village. There was a sombre mood of expectancy in the air, like the lull before a storm. Papa's latest letter contained a hint of trouble brewing. He talked of a black swarm of May bugs hovering over the river. We took that to mean 'Germans'.

Shortly after we received Papa's letter we learned that German troops had broken through our defences at Sedan on 13 May. That worried us, for that was where Papa and Gérard were. We heard how the Stukas first spread panic by divebombing our troops; then the German infantry crossed the river, forming pontoons for the Panzers, the German tanks. Those Panzers cut through the Allied troops like a knife through butter, driving them back to the sea.

Within a week France was beaten.

Maman and I thought about Papa and Gérard all the time.

In the village, the first we saw of real war was column after column of refugees, tired and hungry, clogging the roads: on foot, in prams, on carts, bicycles, motorbikes or in cars. Any way to escape the battle zone. All making for the coast. What for? They could hardly dive into the sea and swim to England!

It was so pitiful to see. Now and then we'd hear the screaming Stukas diving on these poor, defenceless souls, like eagles on their prey. The sky would be black with them. And they'd send the refugees diving into ditches or under wagons. Why, oh, why did they have to gun down old men, women and children?

After the civilians came the soldiers. Stragglers in twos and threes, tens and twelves. Scarcely ever was it an orderly retreat. It was more like every man for himself, grabbing whatever food and drink they could beg, borrow or steal. Those late May days were extremely hot. The soldiers reeled about like drunks in their tiredness and hunger, but worst of all was the thirst.

There wasn't a lot we could do for the retreating army or refugees. Hot on their heels came the Boche, the Germans, chasing them into the sea. The first Germans to pass through the village were Rommel's Panzer Tank Troops. To be fair, they were polite and without any of the arrogance we were to experience later from the SS. Many wore colourful silk scarves round their necks and had long hair; they were so very young.

Mind you, they were very strict about one thing: anyone caught sheltering Allied soldiers would be shot on the spot! Notices in French and German went up all over the countryside. Now we all knew where we stood.


Two days after the enemy tanks had rumbled over the village cobblestones, I noticed something strange. Early that morning, I was doing my rounds – letting out the chickens, collecting eggs, feeding the cows – when all at once I noticed some dark red spots in the yard. I thought it was probably blood from a wounded animal or a hen that had been caught by a fox in the night. I followed the trail across the yard and into the barn. There I found a red pool beneath two straw bales – and the trail petered out.

There was a lot of blood. Only then did it come into my head that it might not be from an animal… The blood might be from a wounded soldier! But who? Friend or foe? English, French or German? And was he still alive?

In a shaky voice, I called out, 'Who's there?'

At first the only sounds were from our farm animals – a loud *cock-a-doodle-do* from a cockerel that made me jump, and several *moos* from the cows in the farmyard. Then I caught the sound of a faint moan. It was coming from the other end of a dark tunnel between two bales of straw.

'Wait there. I'm going to fetch Maman,' I shouted.

That seemed to stir the unknown soldier, if such he was, because a tired voice said, 'No, no, best not.'

So, he was definitely English. But the voice sounded vaguely familiar. His next words clinched it.

'Little Gingernob, it's me.'

'Billy-Tommy!' I cried in surprise and delight.

'Sssh! Keep your row down or you'll give me away. Those Gerries are all over the shop. You could . . . *oooh!*' His voice trailed away into a series of groans. He was clearly in a lot of pain.

I didn't know what to do. But one thing was certain: Maman had to be told – and quickly.

'I don't care what you say,' I told him. 'I'm going for Maman.'

By the time I returned to the barn with Maman, a pair of long legs in muddy brown trousers had appeared through the hole. The rest painfully followed.

We did our best to help him, but he was too heavy for us and slumped to the hay-strewn floor. As he lay there helpless, we soon located the source of the bleeding. His shirt was stained dark red and fresh blood was oozing out above his belt.

'I caught a bullet in the guts,' he muttered through

14

clenched teeth. 'Sorry, my friends, but I think I'm done for. Just bring me a drink of water and leave me be for a few minutes before I make myself scarce; it won't do for me to be found here. I don't want to cause you any bother.'

With that, his eyes closed and he keeled over, out cold.

Neither I, nor Maman gave a thought to danger in aiding the 'enemy'. As best we could we half-carried, half-dragged him across the yard and into the house. He was too bulky to heave up the stairs – and we couldn't leave him in the living-room, what with Germans likely to burst in at any moment. In the end, we decided to make up a mattress with a pillow and blankets in the cellar, between the cider bottles and potato sacks.

'He won't last long unless we get a doctor to him quickly,' Maman said. 'He's lost too much blood. But is it fair to involve someone else?'

'We *must* help him,' I said, tears starting in my eyes. 'We are French and free, not slaves of the Germans. If the doctor wants to come, good for him; that's his lookout.'

Maman agreed and sent me off to the village. Dr Laurent lived at the far end, by the church. He'd retired long before the war, but always turned out, grumbling, for emergencies such as births or deaths.

I rode my rickety old bike down to his house, knowing that every second counted. Luckily, it didn't take long to persuade him. Above all, he was a French patriot. He was the only person in the village with a car, so he spluttered up the hill ahead of me. By the time I arrived home on my bike, he was standing over Billy, shaking his head.

'Not good, not good,' he muttered into his beard after examining the unconscious soldier. 'Quick, hot water, bandages . . . What? No bandages? Tear up an old sheet then. Hurry!'

Unzipping his brown leather bag, he took out some instruments wrapped in an old striped shirt. I turned away – the sight of so much blood made me queasy. Maman was the brave one. She helped tear off the stiff shirt, wash the wound and stem the blood. She even threaded the needle for old Dr Laurent to sew up the stomach flaps.

'Will he survive?' I asked as the doctor was washing the blood off his hands.

He shrugged, turning a wet palm up, then down. Up meant life, down meant death. It was evidently touch and go.

At the door, the doctor turned and put a finger to his lips. We knew what he meant. If the Germans found out we were helping an English soldier, we'd be done for, all of us.

It was a couple of days before Billy came round. We kept him tucked up, nice and warm. Each morning and evening I washed his bristly face; despite the cool cellar, he had a high fever. He had lost so much blood that his pale forehead glistened like marble, and his long, thin hands were chalky white. Once he was back in the land of the living, Maman spooned beef broth and egg custard into his mouth. That seemed to revive him a little, but he was still extremely weak.

With every hour we expected a knock at the door, signalling the arrival of a German search party to turn the house upside down – just like the English had done only a few weeks before. That's the trouble with living under occupation – anyone can come barging in at any time. And you can't even trust your neighbours. That's why we kept our secret to ourselves.

I was so scared. One night I even dreamed of being dragged out of bed to the village square, stood up against the wall of the Town Hall and blindfolded. A dozen soldiers were aiming rifles at my head. I was shouting '*Vive la France!*' as the shots rang out . . .

I woke up with a start. Thank God it was only a dream. Yet the shots were still coming: bang, bang, bang!

It took me a moment to realize it wasn't rifle-fire. It was someone knocking on the door downstairs.

Germans!

Next thing, I heard Maman's nervous voice, 'All right, all right. I'm coming.'

Then I heard the tramping of feet in the yard outside, raised German voices, scraping and banging like furniture being shifted. I hardly dared breathe. Had they discovered Billy in the cellar? Would they shoot me? I buried my head under the covers.

Silence. From under the bedclothes I could hear the stairs creaking; someone was coming towards my room. The door opened, that someone sat on my bed . . . and burst into tears. It was Maman.

I sat up in bed, throwing off the blankets. 'Maman, what is it? What's happened?'

To my astonishment, the tears gave way to a watery grin – like pale sunshine after the rain. That made me cross. 'For Heaven's sake, what's going on?' I cried. 'Should we be laughing or crying?'

'Both,' she said, lowering her voice. 'First the good news. We've still got Billy. They didn't find him, didn't even bother to look.'

'And the bad?'

'We've now got two patients on our hands . . . The second's German!'

*Four*

# Billy's Story

Neither patient was in any condition to carry on the war in our house – not that they were even aware of each other's presence. The German had been blinded and badly burned when his tank blew up. His comrades had patched him up as best they could, bandaging his face, arms and chest, just leaving slits for eyes, nose and mouth. Nose for breathing, mouth for eating, eyes . . . in case he got his eyesight back, I suppose. They had dumped him on us until the field hospital caught up with the advancing troops. The German army was in too much of a hurry to polish off the Allied troops trapped in the pocket around Dunkirk.

Our poor German was in terrible pain, screaming and groaning constantly. There was nothing we could offer but quiet words of comfort. That seemed to help; the sound of a female voice calmed him down, and his initial screams faded to soft moaning, as if he didn't want to show his agony.

The Germans had left a good supply of morphine and other medicine to dull their soldier's pain. Naturally, Dr Laurent shared it between the two wounded men. But, while the German seemed to be getting worse, Billy began to show signs of improvement. There was still no chance of him walking or even sitting up in bed. But he was able to talk in short bursts. Indeed, he was keen to tell us his story. Over the next three days we pieced it together. What an amazing tale it turned out to be.

Billy had been with his regiment in Arras when the Germans broke through the Maginot Line on 11 May. The old market town came in for a real battering from Junkers and Stukas, reducing it to rubble. Those first days of the war in France were an eye-opener for the Allies. For the first time they realized how badly equipped and ill-prepared they were for modern warfare. Many regiments had no anti-tank guns, not enough tanks or trucks. The French even used horse-drawn artillery, from World War I, twenty years before. So, when two hundred Junker 87s screeched down on them at Arras, the poor horses panicked and were slaughtered in just a few hours. German tanks broke through unopposed. Another problem for the Allies was the lack of air protection from the RAF. Where on earth were the British planes?

If that weren't bad enough, French tanks sometimes mistook the British for Germans and fired on them, causing many casualties – and the British returned the compliment. It was total chaos.

Billy found himself cut off from his regiment outside the town. He and a few dozen Welsh Guards were holding on to a cluster of farm buildings on a stretch of the Arras-Givenchy road. All they had were their rifles and several rounds of ammunition.

As Billy told it, a thick mist hung over the canal and flat meadows to the south as he peered through the peephole he had made. His post was in the attic of a farm cottage. All at once, the mist parted and he spotted dust rising from German tanks on the other side of the canal.

The Panzers ground to a halt and Billy watched fascinated as they swung their long gun barrels round to point directly at his cottage. A few seconds later, a shell came crashing through the roof, causing havoc in the attic. Billy tumbled down the stairs and out of the front door as four more shells smashed through the walls. Suddenly there was a crash . . . a shower of tiles and dusty beams . . . a blast of heat bowled him over. In the choking dust he heard a small voice saying, 'I've been hit.'

Then he realized the voice was his own.

It didn't hurt, but his left arm hung useless at his side

and a trickle of blood dripped down from behind his right ear.

'Come on, boy-o, lean on me and we'll leg it to safety.' It was one of the Welsh Guards – he had saved Billy's life. By the time the German tanks crossed the canal, Billy and several other soldiers had made it to an abandoned café further up the road. But how were they to stop the enemy? Suddenly Billy had an idea.

He and his comrades collected china plates from the café and laid them out in patterns across the road, right in the path of the approaching tanks. When the Panzers came nosing down the road, they were clearly puzzled by the white plates. The commander gave a sharp cry, 'Halt! Mines!'

Unaware of the ambush, the crews got out of their tanks and walked forward to inspect the 'minefield'. That was the chance Billy and his friends were waiting for: they opened fire, shooting all the enemy before setting fire to their crewless tanks.

This was only the first of Billy's adventures. Because of his injuries, the remaining soldiers had to leave him. He would have to make his own way back. By this time they'd heard from other fleeing soldiers that the order had come to pull out and retreat to the coast.

Billy cut across country in the rough direction of the Channel ports. On the way he swapped his army tunic for a ragged old jacket from a scarecrow. He ended up at a deserted farmhouse where he hoped to find food. He must have passed out because, when he came to in the barn loft, he heard German voices down below. Luckily, he'd pulled up the ladder so they had no way of climbing up to the top. All the same, he was stuck there all night with the Germans sleeping down below.

Before daybreak he let down the ladder and crept out of the barn while the soldiers were still sleeping. But, just as he was crossing the yard, a guard dog began to bark, alerting the lookout. In a few seconds the whole farm was swarming with Germans, bayonets fixed, prodding every bale of straw and pile of rags. But they didn't find him.

He had burrowed into a big pile of manure in the middle of the yard! If it hadn't been for a rooting pig he might have got away with it. But the pig grabbed his foot, thinking it was a tasty morsel, then ran off honking when Billy kicked its nose. That brought Germans straight to his hiding place and he was dragged before an officer. He knew he could expect no pity. The officer was keen to dispose of him as quickly as possible.

With a spotless white handkerchief held to his nose, the officer demanded to know Billy's rank and battalion. The last thing Billy wanted to own up to was the Coldstream Guards – they were renowned for taking no prisoners in the First World War. He would have been shot on the spot. An eye for an eye. So he 'confessed' to being an Irish freedom fighter on the run from the British for bomb attacks in London.

'Ah,' said the German with a wry smile. 'If you are an Irish patriot, then you speak Irish.'

'Oh, yes,' said Billy. In for a penny, in for a pound. The only Irish he knew was 'blarney', but he remembered the few Scottish words his Uncle George from Aberdeen had taught him: 'Och, 'tis a braw, bricht, moonlicht nicht the nicht, ye no ken? A'm built like a bothy, hefty. A'm all wabbit and crabbit. Ma hale brood tak me for grantit. A'll aye be the wan tae dae it. A'm no masell...' And all in an accent that would have had him strung up by the Highland Regiment!

The 'ochs' and 'ayes', not to mention the stink, were enough for the German officer. In any case, surely no Englishman would have hidden in a pile of cow muck . . . So he told an orderly to douse Billy under the farmyard pump and patch up his wounds. And Billy was on his way, a free man.

Before he left, he built himself a bike from bits and pieces in the abandoned garage; and down the road he cycled, singing, 'It's a long way to Tipperary, it's a long way to go . . .'

But the 'luck of the Irish' didn't hold. Billy's intention was to ride to the coast where he'd heard British ships were taking off refugees. It was a race against time. If he could make it to Dunkirk he might get back to England. He was within some twenty-five kilometres of the old port when he ran into a large company of men, about ninety of them. It turned out they were from the Norfolk Regiment. Safety in numbers, he reckoned. He couldn't have been more wrong.

Soon afterwards they were surrounded by the dreaded Death's Head Division of SS troops. It happened at a village called *Le Paradis*. But it was no paradise for any of the men.

Billy thought, 'that's it, war's over, off to a prisoner-of-war camp.' But the SS were in no mood to take prisoners.

Despite waving a white flag, throwing down their rifles and putting their hands in the air, the men were kicked, beaten and shoved into a field. They assumed that the Germans were going to count and question them, maybe give them some food. To Billy's horror, he suddenly saw two heavy machine guns being trained on the prisoners. The rattle of machine-gun bullets swept the field, back and forth, mowing down the defenceless men. When all that remained was a heap of bloody bodies sprawled on the ground, the SS went round finishing off survivors with bayonets.

Billy led a charmed life. At the first burst of fire he had

flung himself to the ground and was then knocked out by a hefty Norfolker falling on top of him. The poor dead soldier saved his life.

It was pitch dark when Billy came to. In a daze, hardly able to breathe and feeling a raging fire in his stomach, he wondered at first whether he had woken up in hell. But surely hell wasn't damp grass in his mouth and someone's cold face stuck up against his? It took him ages to struggle free of the dead bodies piled on top of him. He could barely stand, was doubled up with pain; it seemed he'd copped a bullet in the stomach.

Just as he was about to crawl into some bushes, he heard the strangest sound. A muffled voice was calling from somewhere far away, 'Help! Help!'

Billy trod a path through the corpses in the darkness, following the faint cries. The sounds led him to a jumbled heap of arms, legs and heads – not all attached to bodies. As best he could, he pulled and heaved human debris out of the way until he'd made a hole big enough for the person who'd called for help to scramble out.

He was only a youngster, a tiny fellow who, miraculously, hadn't a scratch on him.

Without a word of thanks, he looked Billy up and down and muttered, 'Gawd, you're in a bad way, mate. Sorry I can't help.' And with that he took to his heels, running for all he was worth across the fields.

Poor Billy just peered into the gloom, feeling angry. War certainly brings out the worst in some people – and the best in others!

What now? Billy was feeling too weak to walk all the way to Dunkirk. Where was he anyway? The trouble with the British army was that they never seemed to tell you where you were going, how far it was or what you were going to do once you got there! Billy knew from signposts that he'd passed through Givenchy, Messines and St Omer and, from the damp air he sniffed through his squashed nose, he knew he wasn't far from the sea.

If he could only find a senior officer he might locate papers to show him where he was. It wasn't easy in the dead of night to identify an officer, but at last he found a man with one pip on the shoulder of his uniform and a fallen peaked cap. Fortunately, he was still wearing his leather pouch. Not only did Billy discover a map, he found something even more precious – a compass.

As far as Billy could make out, he was north of a place called Bourbourg, not far from the village of Gravelines.

Then it dawned on him. *Gravelines!* That was where his friends lived!

But should he put us at risk? He knew the punishment for harbouring Allied soldiers. Yet if he was going to survive he needed help – only to rest at our farm for a few hours. Perhaps he could cadge some food and a dressing for his wounds. With all the moving about, his stomach wound was now bleeding badly. Once rested and patched up he thought he could somehow make it to Dunkirk and back home to England.

So that's how he got here. Billy's story. One of the many tales of heroism, tragedy and good and bad luck. But how many tales went untold?

*Five*

# Telegrams

If Billy's story did one thing, it brought home to us the horror of war and the cruelty of the enemy. How could we fully understand man's cruelty to man? We who hadn't set foot outside our village, who hadn't seen a battlefield. We felt pity and cared for our English and German patients alike, and found it difficult to hate one and love the other. They were both young and helpless, both totally dependent on us. It was impossible to imagine them, bayonet in hand, stabbing the life out of another human being, stamping on the last spark of another human's existence.

At church on Sunday, Father François didn't rant on about the wickedness of one side or the other. He talked of loving one's enemy, of faith, hope and love. The Allies were Christian nations. Germany and its partner Italy were Christian nations. Surely they all believed in loving fellow humans? The Pope was Italian and he hadn't spoken out for one side or the other.

In our village, Madame Renard at the baker's left no one in any doubt about her views. Adolf Hitler was doing us a service by cleansing Europe of parasites, especially Jews and communists, bringing firm order. In her opinion, that's what we French needed most of all: a strong hand. And anyway, the Germans and Italians were our neighbours, while the English lived across the sea and were our age-old enemy.

At the local café where we delivered our milk, opinion was divided: France needed a strong leader like Hitler, or, France needed another revolution, led by workers. Our Mayor, Monsieur Blanc, sat on the fence, as usual, bending with the wind: 'We mustn't be too hasty in our judgement. Let's wait and see who comes out on top.'

Something happened, however, that decided Maman's and my position, if ever there was any doubt. So far we'd seen the war through others' eyes. We'd watched the coming and going of soldiers through the village – the only difference we could see was the colour of the uniform. One day – I'll never forget the date: 30 May 1940 – we received a telegram.

Now that was an event! An ominous event. Everyone in the village knew what it meant. *Death*. So when the postman cycled down the hill on his bike to deliver the bad news, the whole village knew before we did. Old

Ferdinand, the postman, didn't call with chatty letters at five o'clock in the afternoon.

Maman was in the kitchen baking potato peelings for the chickens; I was out in the meadow milking the cows. The first I knew of the news was Maman running across the field waving a piece of paper in each hand; her dark hair was blowing wildly in the wind, her red face was wet with tears.

At first I thought the war was over and that Maman was crying tears of joy. Every day, we talked about Papa and Gérard coming home, we even half-expected to see them come striding down the road, at any moment, having laid down their arms. Sometimes, when I went into the barn, I even looked around, imagining one or both of them to be hiding in the straw. They were born farmers, after all, not soldiers. Then I suddenly wondered if it could be bad news. About Papa and Gérard.

In the time it took Maman to reach me, I'd swung from wild hope to dark despair, fearing the worst. I wiped my warm, milky hands on my apron and slowly stood up as Maman came near. Her face and first words removed all doubt.

'Our men are dead.'

It's funny how you think of the most stupid things at times like that. The first thought that came into my head was: 'Why bother to send two telegrams when one would do?' After all, they'd died together, on the same day, on more or less the same spot, blown away by a shell.

I soon came to my senses. For the first time, I saw Maman weak and helpless, utterly defeated. A whimper started up somewhere at the back of her throat; it rose in volume to a pitiful wail. The scream must have echoed across fields and woods like the screeching of a flock of crows. Jumbled words tumbled from her mouth.'Who'll till the fields? Gérard's got a place at college. There's no one to continue our name. Why didn't God listen to my prayers? I'll kill those Germans myself, so help me! Papa was going to bring me home some white lace, he promised . . .'

I just plonked myself down on the milking stool and cried my eyes out.

That night Maman couldn't bring herself to go near our German patient. The poor man got no food or milk, not even stale bread and water. *He* was responsible for our grief! I think he must have guessed what was wrong by the sound of our crying. But he saw nothing through his sightless eyes and he didn't say a word. He just turned his bandaged face to the wall.

I had to share my grief with Billy. Not that he was in any state to rise and take revenge on the Germans. But he was clearly very upset for us, letting out a string of words I didn't understand.

★　★　★

The next day, being Sunday, Maman and I went to mass wearing black armbands and dark headscarves. The entire village was there, sharing their sympathy with us. Even those who didn't normally go to church stood outside to murmur their condolences. A little boy pressed some wild flowers into Maman's hands.

Father François gave a moving sermon, mentioning Papa and Gérard as the village's first fallen sons. They were now at rest, safe in God's hands, free from suffering and war . . . Yet when he looked up, his gaze settling on us, his usually kind face twisted into a look of pity mixed with anger. He seemed to speak as a man of the people rather than a man of God. 'This is a tragic day for us and for France. God bids us to love our neighbour, to turn the other cheek. "Thou shalt not kill," He says. But God is wrong. There comes a time when every patriot must stand up for what is right and just. I will *not* stand by and watch our men being taken from us. Whatever happens, the flame of French resistance must not go out.' His voice rose to a defiant shout, *'It will not go out.* France has lost a battle and two of her brave sons. *She will not lose the war!'*

Well, that was one in the eye for Madame Renard at the baker's and the other German-lovers. Good for old François. His words made Maman and me feel a little better. We weren't to know then that he would one day pay for his outspokenness. Madame Renard would see to that.

*Six*

# Good Samaritans

The loss of our loved ones made us even more determined to do what we could to save Billy. We knew that if he didn't get proper treatment for his stomach wound he would probably die. The wound was already starting to give off a worrying smell of rotting flesh. He knew that, too. Without access to proper facilities, all the doctor could do was deaden the pain for a while and change the dressing. All *we* could do was provide food and comfort.

Billy himself kept threatening to leave us 'once I get back on my pins'. He kept worrying about the danger he was putting us in. And once 'our' German was well enough to walk around, he was bound to sniff out the Englishman and give him – and us – away to the hated SS.

We knew from Billy and other refugees that the retreating troops were converging on Dunkirk, some twenty-five kilometres down the coast. The British government had launched a daring rescue attempt, sending hundreds of boats to take off as many soldiers as they could, both British and French. We'd also heard from village gossip that, oddly, Hitler had issued a 'Halt Order' on 24 May. German tanks were to stand fast before Dunkirk and let the *Luftwaffe*, the mighty German air force, have the 'honour' of finishing off the trapped Allied army.

*If* – and it was a very big 'if' – we could somehow get Billy to Dunkirk and on to a ship, we might yet save his life. He'd make it back to England and lie in a nice quiet hospital bed deep in the English countryside – away from guns and bombs and the ever-present fear of a knock at the door. Billy readily agreed, though he wasn't so keen on our involvement.

'I owe my life to you as it is,' he told us. 'I feel stupid just lying here, causing you trouble. If only my darned legs could hold me I'd be off.'

We left it at that. But how were we to get him all the way to Dunkirk? The answer came from an unexpected source. That Sunday evening, we had a visitor. It was Father François. He had come to sit with us in quiet prayer for Papa and Gérard. Not only that. He'd heard of our German 'lodger' and felt it his Christian duty to offer him spiritual comfort. When we admitted that we couldn't stand to look at the man, the priest grew sad.

'My children, *he* isn't responsible for your loss. As a German soldier, it is his duty to fight for his country. Maybe he has a father or brother killed by the Allies. He is, after all, still one of God's children.'

We felt ashamed, and Maman made some warm bread and milk for the hungry man. As his whole face was covered in bandages, we couldn't actually see how he felt. But Maman was surprised when she felt a grateful squeeze on her arm from his good hand.

Since he evidently spoke no French and was too weak to utter more than grunts or groans, his 'conversation' with the priest was all one way. He obviously understood as Father François recited the Lord's Prayer, because at the end of it he muttered, 'Amen,' and touched the priest's hand with the tips of his fingers. The priest drew the sign of the cross on the man's palm and got ready to leave.

We had told no one except the doctor about our secret. So far. But if we were going to save Billy's life we needed help. And surely a priest wouldn't betray our 'confession'. As Maman was showing him out, she took his arm and gently led him towards the barn. There the three of us sat down in the twilight on some straw.

'Father,' Maman began nervously. 'I have to confess something. The German isn't our only patient. We are sheltering an English soldier, down in the cellar. He is badly wounded and could well die unless we do something. We have to get him to Dunkirk somehow. It's his only chance.'

The priest's expression had not altered in the half light. And when Maman had finished, he sat silent, gazing at us partly in surprise, partly in admiration. Then, with a glance upwards, as if seeking God's guidance, he murmured, 'What you are doing is a truly Christian act. You are Good Samaritans. Never pass by on the other side.' He paused. 'But getting him to Dunkirk won't be easy. You'd have to go through road blocks and German patrols. You could well be shot.'

Slowly he fished in the pocket of his long black robe and pulled out a small black cross. In silence he held it up in one hand, closed his eyes and murmured a prayer. Then he sighed, opened his eyes and spoke quietly.

'I'll help you. You have a horse and cart. Put the sick man in the cart and cover him with hay. Madame, you must stay here. We don't want busybodies noticing anything odd; in any case, someone must mind the farm. I'll take Marie. A priest and a young girl will excite less suspicion.'

Getting up and putting the cross back in his pocket, he said finally, 'We'll leave at first light tomorrow.'

We didn't know what to say. He was right, of course.

Our only chance of getting through German lines was to appear as innocent as possible. And what could be more innocent than a horse and hay cart, a pig-tailed girl and a priest? But what if we were discovered? It didn't bear thinking about. What is more, we'd now drawn another human being into danger.

Next day I was up at the crack of dawn, even before the first cock-crow. Maman had already woken Billy and told him the news as she spooned some beef broth past his lips. 'It's going to be painful for you in our old cart, rattling over the cobblestones. And it may all be in vain if you're caught. But what else can we do . . . ?'

She shrugged. Billy nodded.

In the meantime, I had rigged up a makeshift stretcher from two long poles and some canvas sacking. By the time the priest arrived, I had the cart ready. Didon, our old farm horse, was patiently waiting to plod wherever he was told.

With much puffing and blowing, Maman and the priest got Billy's bag of bones on to the stretcher, up the cellar steps and into the cart. As we tossed old potato sacks and armfuls of hay over him, Billy suddenly scared us by letting out a loud sneeze. This was followed by a muffled voice. 'Sorry. I forgot to say I suffer from hayfever.'

Maman was unsympathetic. 'Cross your legs and pinch

your nose. If you sneeze when there are Germans within earshot you'll get us all killed. Remember that.'

Billy nodded and lay back under his pile of hay.

*Seven*

# An Encounter with the SS

In the days leading up to our escape bid, I'd tuned in with Maman to the BBC World Service. 'This is London calling . . .' So we knew that Britain had a new Prime Minister, Winston Churchill. He had promised nothing but 'blood, toil, tears and sweat'. There were to be no more rosy pictures of heroic warfare from the 'umbrella man', as we called the previous Prime Minister, Neville Chamberlain. If that message wasn't blunt enough, the surrender of Holland and Belgium on 27 and 28 May made things plain. We could expect no outside help. France was doomed.

So when we jolted along the road to Dunkirk that June morning we knew that most of Europe was under the Nazi jackboot. As Nazi chiefs boasted: 'The war is won; all that is left is to finish it.' Where would it all end? Was any nation strong enough to resist Hitler? With America and Russia keeping out of the war, it looked like Britain's fate was sealed, too. Poor Billy. Even if he got home safely, it would only be a matter of time before the Germans landed.

We passed German ambulances taking casualties in the opposite direction, and saw the occasional work brigade of mainly Polish prisoners-of-war – digging trenches, working in the fields, repairing bomb-damaged bridges and canals. Otherwise, the roads were fairly quiet, the houses mostly deserted, the farms empty, apart from stray dogs, whining and looking for their owners.

Where had all the refugees gone, with their carts and prams and pitiful belongings?

The road took us inland to the village of Bourbourg. So far, so good. No one had stopped us or even paid us much attention. If it wasn't for the constant whirr of German planes overhead, we wouldn't have known that somewhere close – no more than a few kilometres away – people were being blown to pieces.

As we entered the village, Father François muttered under his breath, for Billy's benefit, 'There's a German patrol up ahead . . . SS troops by the look of their uniforms. Don't move a muscle and, for God's sake, don't sneeze!'

Sure enough, the soldiers blocked the road and waved us down. 'Halt!'

Two grim-faced sentries shouted at us in German.

When we didn't respond, they poked the old priest in the ribs with their guns. The message was clear: Get down or get shot!

We got off the cart and stood in the road, our hearts in our mouths. The men fixed bayonets and climbed on to the cart. I held my breath. Surely it was all over!

The first soldier jabbed his bayonet hard into the hay at the back of the cart. The other clambered into the front where Billy lay under the heap of hay.

I already knew that Billy led a charmed life. And, miraculously, his luck worked its magic yet again. Just as the second soldier went to thrust the sharp blade into the hay, his attention suddenly turned to a new arrival. Behind us, honking his horn, was an English army chaplain in a dusty old motor car.

'I say, chaps,' he called breezily. 'Clear the way, will you? I've got a boat to catch.'

The Germans all stood and stared, totally unamused by this officer's swagger. His arrival in army uniform and dog collar had evidently caught the SS off guard. But they soon recovered themselves. After all, they were in charge here, not him and he had to be taught a lesson!

'Name?' shouted an SS officer, going up to the car.

'Name? Oh, I see,' the Englishman said casually. He took out a cigarette case and offered a cigarette to the officer. 'I'm Temporary Chaplain the Reverend Reginald

Podmore. Seem to have lost my way, got left behind. But I'm not a fighting man, so clear the way, old sport, and I'll be off.'

The German clearly wasn't an 'old sport'. He stepped back and issued a sharp order to his men. Next moment a hail of bullets riddled the car's shiny black carriage. We stood there, horrified. Slowly, the door swung open and the chaplain slumped on to the pavement. He was still breathing, his ruddy face bearing a look of astonishment.

Father François immediately rushed to the dying man's aid as he lay there, half in the gutter. But a line of soldiers barred his way. It wouldn't do for the chaplain to live and report the shooting of a non-fighting soldier.

I couldn't take in what I'd witnessed. How could they shoot the man in cold blood? They called themselves Christians! How could they fire on a man of God?

All the same, his misfortune was our good luck. Having satisfied their blood-lust for the moment, the SS patrol waved us on. It was just as well they didn't catch the bout of sneezing coming from under the hay.

When we were out of earshot, I reported to Billy all we'd seen. He just sighed deeply. 'That's war,' he said. 'And that's the SS.' Then he added, 'What a nitwit!'

Once past Bourbourg, we made for Bergues, on the outskirts of Dunkirk. We were now out of German-occupied territory and inside what was called the Allied Escape Corridor, a narrow strip of land leading to the coast. Our progress was painfully slow because the road was choked with soldiers trying to reach the port. To make matters worse, the closer we got to Dunkirk, the more terrifying the air bombardment became. Messerschmitts, Dorniers and Stukas repeatedly swept the road with bullets and dropped their bombs, leaving the dead and dying strewn across the sand-dunes and sea grass beside the road.

I'd once heard someone say that each bomb had someone's name on it. Maybe the Germans didn't know our names, since we survived.

During one raid, we halted beneath an old chestnut tree in the bend of the road. All at once, a car-load of people drove up, honking and shouting. The driver – a red-faced man in a black suit and bowler hat – screamed at us, 'Move along! We need this shelter more than you peasants!'

When we didn't budge, the car hit us from behind, scaring Didon into a gallop. Father François let out a string of words I never thought he knew . . .

We were left stranded in the open, some fifty metres on. It was too late to make a dash for safety. Six planes were bearing down on us, their guns spitting fire.

'Quick, Marie, under the wagon!' Father François

shouted. Billy would have to take his chances.

Just in time, we scrambled underneath the old cart. We heard the phut-phut-phut of bullets and saw dirt spurt up beside the track, like jets of water. Then a huge bang blasted our eardrums; it was followed by further, more distant explosions – and screams. Then came a searing, red-hot wind and the loud patter of raining stones.

Poor Didon let out a terrifying shriek and would have bolted had there been anywhere to go. But the road in front and behind was blocked by a long line of refugees. Panic-stricken, the old horse reared up on his hind legs, pawing the air and throwing Billy to the back of the cart, against the tailboard.

Then all grew still. The planes roared on, the dust began to settle, shrapnel stopped falling, and we poked out our heads to survey the damage. Our first concern was Billy. But apart from straw stuffed up his nose and down his throat, he was as right as rain.

It was the priest who first spotted that something was wrong. He spotted a boot lying in the cart near Billy. Hastily, he picked it up and tossed it away. I watched the boot's flight into a ditch . . . where it tipped out its bloody contents. I glanced back at the chestnut tree. It wouldn't be producing any chestnuts this year . . . The tree and the car beneath it had completely vanished, leaving just a smoking crater in the road.

'God rest their souls!' muttered the priest.

Our old carthorse wasn't used to such a racket. Now that he'd recovered from the shock, his eyes grew wild, his nostrils flared, his mouth frothed and foamed. It took all our strength to stop him bolting across the dunes and into one of the many drainage channels.

It took us two days to cover fifteen kilometres. But at last, on the morning of 3 June, we struggled up a hill to the west of Dunkirk and, on the crest, stared down at the most astonishing sight I'd ever seen.

Instead of the ancient town with its narrow alleyways and quaint old houses, there stretched a massive pile of grey dusty rubble, lit up here and there by orangey-red fires. When I was nine, Papa had taken me to the fifteenth-century church of St Eloi for my confirmation. Now the church was just a smouldering ruin. It had stood firm against attacks and the elements for over five hundred years – and been destroyed in minutes by high explosives. The only recognizable monument was the statue to Jean Bart, the famous Corsair pirate. He was still sticking out his chest and facing the enemy defiantly, as if ready to run them through with his cutlass.

But it was the harbour that mostly caught our attention. We had to let Billy share our joy. Propping him up between us, we stared down, misty-eyed, at the one remaining corner of free France. As far out as the eye could see the water was dotted with boats, French and British, of all shapes and sizes.

There were long grey destroyers and the famous 'Smoky Joe' minesweepers, dwarfing the 'cockleshell' boats – Thames barges, weekend yachts, Dutch scoots and Portsmouth tugs. There were ferryboats, too: *Puffing Billy* from Hayling, the *Maids* – of Kent, Brighton and Canterbury; the *Yorkshire Lass* trawler from Grimsby, the cross-channel steamers and Irish Sea ferries; the paddle steamer *Princess Elizabeth*. Simply hundreds of them. All were flying the white ensign and waiting their turn to enter the harbour. The bigger ships would be tying up alongside the two wooden piers that stretched into the sea like two crab claws.

It seemed that they were waiting for nightfall before entering the harbour. The reason was terrifyingly obvious. Up above us wave upon wave of German planes were roaring by, dropping fire bombs and machine-gunning anything that moved on shore or pier.

Not that they had it all their own way. The sky was a patchwork quilt of black and grey smoke trails from stricken planes tumbling into the sea; lines of little grey clouds that exploded like fireworks, then swiftly melted away; bright silver tracer bullets that climbed up the curtain of the sky and burst like rockets into empty space.

It was cheering to see the red, white and blue circles on RAF fuselages, as the Spitfires, Hawker Hurricanes and slow-flying Lysanders did battle with the sinister black-cross vultures of the enemy.

As Billy gazed down, he gave a toothy grin. 'We made it, Little Gingernob!' he said.

Father François decided against the road through town – it was too hazardous. 'We'll take to the beach and see if we can make our way across the sand-dunes.'

The gritty sand made the going tough for poor old Didon. But at least the way was clear of car and lorry debris. We had the sandy path to ourselves. Now and then the wheels of the cart got stuck in the shelves of sand, so we had to dismount and push. It was lucky we'd brought plenty of hay; it certainly came in useful to put under the wheels, making it easier to haul the cart out of sand ruts. We kept as close as we could to the sea, since the wet sand and seaweed helped the cart move more easily.

The water was full of squishy jellyfish, millions of them, each about the size of a man's hand. In the centre of each one was a greenish pattern exactly like a four-leafed clover. 'Your good-luck sign is even in the jellyfish!' I called back to Billy, who had removed the hay and was breathing in the sea air.

He managed to raise himself on one arm to take a look.

But he had seen something else, for he let out a cry and sank back on to the board. Then I saw it, too. At first I thought it was only driftwood bobbing in the swirling tide. Yet as I looked closer I saw it was a soldier's two feet. The toes of his boots were pointing towards the land he had come to defend and for which he'd lost his life.

As we came closer to the harbour, more awful waste of war revealed itself along the shoreline. In the water floated empty life rafts and belts, ration boxes and even oranges.

Other things floated in the sea, too. They stretched in a thin line, just like a high-water mark, all the way along the beach. These were the personal belongings that would never be reclaimed by those who'd fought and died. There in a jumbled row were soldiers' packs. There were socks and shoe polish, toothbrushes and razors, sewing kits, diaries, bibles and leather-bound books. There were the latest letters from home, snapshots of families back in England, staring up at us from the sand. There were bloody, abandoned boots. The most common items were packs of cigarettes: cartons by the thousand, water-soaked and all spilling out in a soggy mass.

A scruffy brown-and-white dog was on the beach, still pitifully searching for his master. He ran along the water's edge, near a boat that lay twisted and half-sunk at the waterline. The dog barked as we jolted past, trotting eagerly alongside Didon for a few yards and then, sensing himself unwanted, running back to wait in vain for his own master at the empty boat.

It must have been getting on for eight o'clock in the evening when we arrived at the harbour, just short of the Western Mole, as the pier was called. Fortunately, much of the day had been overcast, with banks of low-lying cloud. This had hampered enemy planes, sparing us from the worst of the bombing.

A shore party of sailors was shouting orders and directions. 'Form up in ranks! Lay out the dead! Watch for bomb craters! Wounded to the front!'

A lane along the Mole was kept open for stretcher bearers. But there was no time or space for the dead. Tonight was the last chance to evacuate the armies; the order had gone out to all ships and boats. So the dead were tipped off the Mole and into the sea or on to the pilings below.

Father François tied Didon to one of the harbour pilings and we set about getting Billy down from the cart. It wasn't easy and it must have caused him absolute agony. In the last few hours he'd begun to tremble uncontrollably. The priest took the stretcher poles by his head and tipped him forward, half shoving, half lifting, so that the other end of the stretcher overlapped the backboard. With Billy stifling a groan, I grabbed the poles with my back to the cart and we lifted him off.

'This way, Miss,' somebody said. 'The beach is two hundred yards ahead.'

We managed to get Billy to the water's edge where lifeboats lay waiting, rubbing gently against the sand. They were to row out to *HMS Imogen*, which was tied up in deep water at the end of the Mole.

An officer in a naval greatcoat shouted out, 'Walking wounded – For-*ward!*'

All along the beach, men rose from stretchers, limped, hobbled, even crawled to the lifeboats. Some used old spars and oars as crutches, knowing this was their last chance of escape.

As the naval officer came abreast of us, he asked Billy, 'Can you get off the stretcher?'

Billy put all his strength into an effort to rise, but sank back in pain.

'No, sir, I don't think so.'

'Well, I'm sorry, son,' the man said. 'We can't help you. Your stretcher would take up the places of four men. Orders are: only those who can stand or sit up.'

And he passed on.

So near and yet so far. After all Billy had been through . . . I'd never seen a man cry. Now, after all our efforts, after all his hopes had been dashed, Billy gave way.

He was still crying when we reached the cart. Then, just as suddenly, he stopped and lay silent.

When we were climbing up the hill, we heard a quiet voice behind us, 'Sorry, Marie. Sorry, Father. Worse things happen at sea, don't they? My luck's run out at last.'

He was right. And he was wrong.

By the time we reached the brow of the hill, the full moon had sailed out, drawing aside the curtain of cloud. It was now a bright, starry night and we could see the harbour clearly.

In the distance, *HMS Imogen* was sailing peacefully on her way home. Almost without thinking, I raised my arm and waved farewell. Next moment, I froze. A German aircraft, a Dornier 17 I think it was, came diving out of the sky and headed out to sea. It dropped its load of bombs above the ship. We watched in horror as they splashed harmlessly into the sea about the vessel, causing nothing but big waves.

All except one.

That 'lucky' bomb fell right down the funnel of the ship. For a split second there was dead silence. Then an almighty explosion shook the doomed vessel from bow to stern. It shuddered, rose out of the water, its back broken, then sank below the waves, taking its helpless human cargo with it.

'God have mercy on their souls,' murmured the priest. We turned and headed for home.

*Eight*

# The Return Home

The return journey was gloomy, but uneventful. None of us felt like talking. Any Germans we bumped into on the way were unconcerned with us, they were even civil and smiling. I guess the 'Greatest victory of the war', as Hitler termed the German triumph at Dunkirk, made them feel smug – as if they'd won the war already. All that remained, it seemed, was the mopping up.

German troops had reached the Atlantic in the west, the Mediterranean in the south, and the Baltic in the north. Only Britain was left; and now it stood alone. One day Hitler would pay for allowing so many soldiers to escape from Dunkirk. For the moment, however, he had other concerns: hundreds and thousands of prisoners on his hands.

All we had were two wounded men.

Maman was relieved to see us return safe and sound. Of course, she was sorry for Billy. After Father François had hurried off to church, hoping he hadn't been missed, Maman made a fuss of our returning 'prodigal son'.

'Now, Billy-boy,' she said brightly as he lay on the table, 'we're going to put you upstairs in Marie's room. You'll get lots of sunshine there and be able to look out over the countryside. I'll tell you what: I'm going to make you a sponge cake with my special plum jam. What do you think of that?'

Maybe it was his feelings for a fellow soldier and their common suffering, but Billy surprised her by asking, 'How's the German?'

Since we didn't think that Billy would be coming back from Dunkirk, Father François and I didn't see any harm in telling Billy on the way about our German patient.

'Oh, don't worry about him. I've shifted him down to the cellar, out of sight. Now, how about a welcome home drink – some brandy? It'll put the colour back in your cheeks.'

But Billy persisted.'Is he any better?'

Maman didn't understand. Why this sudden interest in the enemy?

'I don't know. I don't want to know. He doesn't speak French, so I've no way of knowing how he is. The sooner they come for him – or the sooner he conks out –

the better. Billy, don't you realize he could give you, and us, away?'

Billy changed the subject. 'You're very kind, Madame. I'm sure Marie's bedroom will be a tonic. But if you don't mind, I'll turn in. It's been a tiring few days.'

'Of course, of course. Marie, help me get Billy upstairs.'

That was easier said than done. But we managed. And an hour later Billy was tucked up in my bed, not exactly sleeping peacefully, but taking cat-naps between spasms of pain. He hadn't had any pain-killing drugs for four days. Dr Laurent was due in the morning; he'd be able to give Billy some relief and tell us if the hay ride had done much damage.

Then Maman told me some disturbing news. 'The Boche are here. Their commandant has taken over the Town Hall – with the mayor's blessing, of course! And the creepy-crawlies have come out of the woodwork – welcoming our 'saviours', hanging out German flags, inviting them home, even providing lists of 'unreliables' – Jews and communists. We must be extra careful from now on. For the moment, we're in their good books as 'helpers', looking after their wounded comrade. One false step though . . .'

That night I slept with Maman in her double bed. I was dead tired and glad of a good night's sleep after the Dunkirk journey. But even in my dreams the terrible image of that ship going down with all hands haunted me.

When I awoke, Maman was already up, talking to someone downstairs. From the low growl I could tell it was old Dr Laurent. He'd examined both patients and seemed far from happy. I could catch his words drifting up the stairs: he was partially deaf and spoke louder than he realized.

'One has gangrene, the other second-degree burns. If either recovers it will be a miracle.'

For a few moments Maman was silent. I could imagine her biting her lip. 'How long have they got?' she said at last.

'God knows. If the pair last out the month I'll be surprised. All I can do is pump them full of morphine and hope the beggars don't suffer too much.'

When the doctor had gone, I got dressed quickly and was just about to go downstairs when I heard Billy calling. He must have overheard the doctor's gloomy verdict.

When I entered his room, he put on a brave face.

'Marie, if I'm soon to be a goner, I want you to do something for me. Write a letter to my mum and dad, there's a good girl. When this lot's over, who knows, you might even meet them. Then you can tell them our story.' He tried to smile, but the drugs seemed to have made him woozy, and he went straight off to sleep.

Maman and I didn't talk about the doctor's visit. We both had our farm chores to see to. As it was, I'd got up late. I could hear the cows calling me: 'Ma-*arie!* Ma-*arie!*' Maman had been summoned with other villagers to the German commandant. So our two sleeping beauties were left alone for a few hours.

It was mid-morning by the time I got back to the house with my milk pails. I was surprised to hear the floorboards creaking above my head. At first I thought it was Billy, stretching his legs. Then a cold shiver went down my spine. Billy couldn't walk. He couldn't even crawl off the stretcher on Dunkirk beach!

So who was upstairs in the bedroom?

A low murmur of voices could be heard. One, tired and slow; the other, more of a grunt, as if the man found speaking difficult. I crept to the foot of the stairs and strained my ears. Billy's voice was instantly recognizable.

'So how d'you feel now?'

Who was he talking to in English? He sounded friendly enough. The 'grunter' replied. I guessed he was saying something like, 'Not so good.'

'Where are your mates? Have you a mother back home?'

I didn't speak German, but I could tell what it was from the, '*Ja, ja*,' and low throat sounds – his mother was alive. He had a wife and two children, as far as I could make out.

He must have shown Billy a photo, because I heard Billy say cheerily, 'Pretty lass. My, my, what bonny kiddies. What are their names?'

That seemed too difficult for the German. He kept repeating after Billy, 'Kiddies . . . Names . . .'

'You know, Jack and Jill, Fritz, Adolf . . .'

A snort came from the German, as if he could only talk through his throat. His wife's name was Anna, his children Erich and Else.

He must have asked Billy if he had any children, because Billy said, 'No, not that I know of, like.' He gave a laugh, then grew serious. 'You and me, chum, we're in the same boat. Far from home and our loved ones. I'm not going to make it. Even if you give me away it won't matter to me. But it will to the good women in this house. Spare them that, comrade. Spare them that.'

By this time I'd crept up the stairs and stood peering through the door. There was our German patient, sitting on Billy's bed, his bandaged head pointed at the window. Somehow he must have got wind of Billy's presence and hauled himself up the stairs. They say a blind man develops other keen senses. Maybe he'd followed his nose . . .

At Billy's words, the German fumbled for his hand. He grasped it firmly. The gesture seemed to promise: 'I won't give them away!'

At that he painfully got to his feet as I scuttled back downstairs. I hid in the kitchen as the heavy steps trudged slowly down the stairs, pausing at the bottom, then heading for the cellar door. Too late, I saw my milk pails blocking his way. He was walking straight for them . . .

'Stop!' I cried.

The poor man could not have had a worse fright if the enemy had stuck a rifle in his back.

'Wait, I'll help you,' I said in a gentler tone.

I took his arm and, instead of leading him down into the cellar, sat him down at the table.

'Now that you're up and about,' I said, 'you might as well have a drink. Here.'

I put a bowl of fresh milk into his hands.

'*Danke, Fräulein Marie.*'

'Oh, so you know my name, do you?' I said, hiding a grin. 'A proper old spy, aren't you? And what's your name?'

I spoke French as I knew no German, and he knew no French or English. Following Billy's example, I listed a few names. Then I said slowly, 'I'm Marie. Who . . . are . . . you?'

He nodded. 'Helmut. Helmut Kruger.'

I took his good hand in mine. 'Good to meet you, Helmut,' I said.

With an effort, he repeated my words, 'Good . . . to . . . meet . . . you, Mademoiselle Marie.'

I laughed. From upstairs I heard a voice call down, 'Now don't you get too fresh with our Helmut or I'll be jealous.'

Not long after I'd seen Helmut back to his bed, Maman came home.

'We'd better tidy up,' she said. 'The commandant will be here at midday. He wants a chat with our unwanted guest. Come on, there's no sense moving Billy again. If they go poking around, too bad.'

Maman was so flustered, I didn't have a chance to tell her of the strange events while she'd been out. Instead, I popped upstairs to warn Billy of the German's arrival.

Dead on twelve o'clock, a car drew up and a young officer marched smartly up to the front door where Maman and I were waiting. He clicked his heels and saluted. Despite the warm day, he was wearing a long, black leather coat and black gloves.

'Hello, ladies,' he said in good French. 'Please take me to your patient.'

We didn't ask which one! But I felt sure it wouldn't be long before our secret was out. Helmut was certain to tell all to his superior. It was his duty.

About an hour later, the officer emerged from the cellar, a grim smile on his face. Without invitation, he sat himself down at the kitchen table and helped himself to a biscuit. As Maman made coffee, he said gravely, 'Well, Madame, I've had an interesting chat with my soldier. He's a brave man. He tells me you have been most kind to him. I want to thank you. Those who aid the German Reich will be rewarded.'

Maman was never one for holding her tongue. She put his bowl of coffee before him before saying calmly, 'I will never aid your Reich. You have killed my only son and my husband. You have occupied my country. I am proud to be French and your enemy. My aid to a wounded soldier is no more than my Christian duty.'

The officer smiled as he sipped his coffee. 'So be it, Madame,' he said grimly. 'Make sure you keep him alive.' He drank his coffee in strained silence.

Only when the car drove away did I breathe a sigh of relief. So Helmut hadn't betrayed us, after all!

I told Maman the whole story. She smiled warmly.

'So there *is* some goodness left in the world,' she murmured.

When I'd got back from feeding Didon and churning the butter, I came in to another surprise. Maman had made up a bed on the sofa in the living-room. Helmut was sitting up, listening to German songs on the wireless.

# Nine

## Friend or Foe?

So here we were: French, English and German; friend and foe – all living together under the same roof. It was wartime. Yet we got on famously. In the evenings we'd often sit round Billy's bed, playing cards. We couldn't play 'Snap' or 'Brag'; it would have put poor Helmut at a disadvantage, as he couldn't see the cards. But we paired him up with Billy who helped him in 'Gin Rummy' and 'Whist', and we had a great time.

Funnily enough, the game he used to beat us easily at was 'Memories'. He seemed to have a sixth sense, diving on just the right card every time. We teased him that he was only pretending not to see.

I wrote Billy's letter for him – but I didn't send it. How could I? It would have to wait till the war was over. Later, when Hitler's luck had turned, I passed it to a Scots soldier who promised to post it when he got back home. I've no idea whether it ever reached its destination.

I never heard from any of Billy's family, even though I put our address on the back.

There isn't a lot left to tell.

All over France, the occupation set French against French. Most kept their noses clean. Some had no choice: they were rounded up, marched off and shot or sent to a camp. But there were those who threw in their lot with the Germans. They were snakes in the grass; you couldn't trust them at all. Anyone they had a grudge against or they suspected of 'anti-German feelings' they gave away to the SS. That's how our dear priest, Father François, got dragged out in the middle of the night – they didn't dare do it in the daytime! One moment he was here, the next he was gone.

We never saw him again. He probably disappeared into one of the German concentration camps. Of course, we all knew who must have betrayed him – that village gossip Madame Renard. Yet no one said a word. Fear ruled the village.

Mind you, not all those who sided with the Germans did so for political reasons. We had a young girl in the village who fell in love with a German soldier billeted on her family. After the war, a group of our boys set upon her, shaved off her hair and paraded her down the village street with a placard round her neck, on which was written the word *Collaborator*. They were tough times.

Some patriots joined the Resistance. They did what they could to make life uncomfortable for the Boche – blowing up arms dumps, cutting telephone wires, sabotaging trucks and cars; they even killed Germans who ventured out alone.

One night in early June we had a visit from a woman I'd never seen around the village. She told us she was from the French Resistance. She was in her early twenties, with dark hair, wearing a black beret and long grey coat. Maybe in peacetime she'd been pretty; but now her mouth was cruel and her look hard.

Pointing to our German patient, she said coldly, 'We know about him. Our people need to question this man, to find out what he knows.'

Maman was taken aback. 'But he knows nothing.'

'How do you know? Was he in Rommel's Panzers?'

Maman shrugged. 'All I know is he got badly burned when his tank blew up.'

'There you are then. He was tank crew. He could be valuable to us, tell us about tank strength and movements, that sort of thing.'

Maman clearly didn't know what to say. The woman left, promising to return. Next evening she was back with another woman, slightly older, talking in an odd dialect, as if she were from the north-east, around Alsace. The two women ignored us, drawing up chairs in front of the sofa. They were obviously not here to have a cosy chat. All at once, one of them drew a knife and waved it before the eye slits in his bandages. Her companion spoke harshly to him in German.

This shocked and frightened us. Immediately Maman went to help Helmut.

But the woman waved the knife towards her, saying sharply, 'Don't interfere or you and your daughter will suffer. What we do is for France.'

'But he's sick,' said Maman in begging tones. 'Don't hurt him. He saved our lives.'

'Oh, yeah. That's what the Germans are here for, I suppose – to save our lives. Go upstairs and keep quiet!'

We could see she meant business.

'Come on, Maman,' I said urgently. 'We'd better do as she says.'

Before we climbed the stairs, Maman brushed past the two women and put her hand on Helmut's arm as if to reassure him or, at least, to show him it wasn't our doing. Once in the bedroom, we sat on the bed, waiting anxiously for the interrogation to finish.

At last, we heard chairs scraping, angry shouts and the sounds of a struggle. Rushing down the stairs, we were just in time to see the women dragging Helmut towards the door. He was trying to cling on to whatever came to hand.

'What on earth are you doing?' Maman screamed. 'Leave him alone!'

'You don't think we can let him live, do you?' the first woman said. 'He's seen us. He'll betray us to the commandant. You'd be in grave danger yourselves.'

Maman stared. 'Don't you know he's blind?'

Now it was their turn to stare. They obviously hadn't realized. But the older woman shrugged and said, 'Never mind, he'll still talk. He'll give us all away.'

They pulled open the door and dragged him through it. Then, all of a sudden, they stood frozen in the doorway, staring past us. We swung round and could hardly believe our eyes.

We saw a figure in a long flannel nightgown, his face as white as a ghost; he was holding our old shotgun in his hands and propping himself up against the wall. It was Billy. Goodness knows how he got himself down the stairs . . .

'Let him go or I'll shoot!' he said firmly.

I ran to Helmut, took his arm and led him back to the sofa.

'Sit down, please,' said Billy to the two women. 'I'm going to tell you a thing or two about war.'

The older woman whispered in the other's ear,

translating Billy's words. The other looked stunned, realizing for the first time that the man with the gun was English, not German.

'Madame,' said Billy to Maman, 'be so kind as to give these ladies a stiff drink. They deserve it. I can see they're bold and fearless. Brainy, too, by the look of them. But they lack something.'

'Oh, what's that?' asked the older woman sarcastically.

Billy put down the shotgun and tapped his chest.

'Heart, Madame, heart. War can be cruel, I should know. I've seen more killing than you've probably had hot dinners. So I've good cause to hate Hitler and the Nazis.'

He paused for the translation.

'But there's another side to war that's rarely spoken of. We're all taught to hate our enemy. Yet he isn't always what he seems. Take Helmut here. He's German. So he's the enemy. You'd shoot him without blinking, wouldn't you. You wouldn't ask: "Is he a good man or a bad man? Is he kind or cruel?" '

Again he waited for his words to sink in. But this time he doubled up in pain, clutching his stomach. I rushed over to him, begging him to go back to bed. Instead, he put his arm round my shoulders, leaning on me for support.

'Ta, love,' he said, 'but I've got to spit it out.'

To the women he said, 'Did you ask anyone here about Helmut? No, you were too sure of yourselves and your enemy. Well, let me tell you something. If it weren't for Helmut, I'd be a dead man. If it weren't for Helmut, this young girl would have been shot. If it weren't for Helmut, her mother would have been executed for sheltering an English soldier. He kept his mouth shut. Why? Out of loyalty to *us*. Not to the Nazis. Not to *his* side. Simply because he cares more for us – his so-called enemies!'

I felt the full weight of his body collapse on me. Together we tumbled to the floor in a heap before anyone could help. It was Helmut who moved first to our aid. He had sat there scared stiff, thinking his end had come, his head moving from Billy to the translator, not taking in a word. Yet understanding everything.

He felt for my arm and, with one bandaged hand, pulled me up and sat me down on the sofa. Maman seemed too overcome to move. As for the two women, they stared down at the table in silence.

'He's dying,' murmured Maman. 'We've been looking after him.'

The two women rose awkwardly from the table, opened the door and left without a word. We never saw them again.

Somehow, Maman and Helmut got Billy back upstairs and into bed.

Billy died early the next morning. Oddly, a few minutes before, he had opened his eyes and looked in turn at each of us sitting round his bed – first me, next Maman, then Helmut. And he smiled.

I took Helmut's hand in mine and drew a cross on his palm. He understood. He remained still for a while. Then his whole body shook with sobs. Unconnected words mingled with the sobs. All I could make out was 'comrade' – *Kamerade,* and 'friend' – *Freund.* Then came angry cries as he beat his fists on his knees.

We thought that Helmut was on the mend. Yet after Billy's death he took to his bed and seemed to lose the will to live. Dr Laurent was right in his forecast, after all. Helmut died on 30 June, at night, no doubt so as not to disturb us.

Neither of our patients saw in the new month. Nor did they live to see the war's end five years later . . .

*Ten*

# Rose Bushes

Gran sighed deeply, her green eyes and thoughts far away. Then, she threw up her hands and said brightly, 'So there you are, my dears, that's my story.'

The two children sat quietly for a few moments. Then Anne-Marie said, 'You promised to show us something interesting before we leave.'

'Oh, so I did, so I did. Follow me. We must hurry before it gets dark,' she said.

On a hill, at the end of the village, stood a church of grey stone, its spire towering over the cluster of houses with TV aerials and dark grey dishes. The grey-haired woman strode down the path that circled the church and led to the graveyard beyond. Struggling to keep up, Anne-Marie and Marcel walked quickly past headstones bearing faded photos of the dead and unkempt graves until they reached a tall poplar tree in a shady corner. It stood as straight as any sentry, on guard over the dead.

Unlike the other graves, the two corner plots were as neat and tidy as a bowling green, each with a stone of white marble at their head. Two rose bushes grew at their feet, their branches intertwining, like hands clasped in friendship.

It was Marcel who first spotted the name:

### BILLY LANGLEY
*An English Soldier*

No date. No age.

The two children felt the cold, rough stone as if it were the English soldier's hand. They put their noses to the flowers and breathed in the fresh, fragrant smell.

'This must be the German's grave,' said Marcel, switching attention to the second plot. He read out the inscription:

### HELMUT KRUGER
*A German Soldier*

Again, no date. No age.

'Enemies in war. Comrades in life. Friends in death,' said Gran.

'Why aren't they buried in the war cemetery?' asked Anne-Marie. 'They were soldiers in the war.'

'So they were, my dear. But somehow I think they would prefer to be side by side, don't you?'

They walked slowly home through the gathering dusk. They each had their own private thoughts: of Billy and Helmut, of a little girl in ginger plaits, and of war that makes some men enemies, but makes other men friends.

# Historical Notes

Although the central characters of this story are fictional, the events portrayed are based on actual incidents: the Dunkirk Evacuation, the sinking of *HMS Imogen,* the SS massacre of 96 Norfolk Regiment soldiers and the killing of the Reverend Reginald Podmore. Even the searching of the nuns, the washing line suspicion and the laying out of china plates as 'mines' actually occurred.

As far as possible, real events and names have been retained.

After the Dunkirk Evacuation, the German ring round France was closed and German victory over France was complete. The French government, under 84-year-old Marshall Henri Pétain, followed a policy of loyal collaboration with the Germans. Some French, however, continued the war. A junior officer, Charles de Gaulle, escaped to London to lead the Free French and form a government in exile. It is his words, spoken on 18 June 1940, that Father François speaks: 'France has lost a battle. She has not lost the war.'

The war continued for another five years, spreading to all of Europe when the Nazis invaded the Soviet Union in June 1941. When Japan joined the Axis Powers (Germany and her allies) and attacked the US fleet at Pearl Harbor in December 1941, the war became truly a *world* war.

The tide began to turn in late 1942 when the Soviet Red Army defeated the Germans at Stalingrad. Gradually the Nazi army was pushed back. And when the joint British-US forces opened a second front by landing on France's Normandy beaches in June 1944 (known as the Normandy Landings), Hitler's armies were caught between the Red Army in the east and the Normandy invasion army in the west.

The war in Europe ended in Allied victory and German defeat in May 1945.

# Further Information

If you would like to find out more about the Second World War, these books will help:

Robin Cross, *Children and War* (Hodder Wayland, 1994)

Robin Cross, *Victims of War* (Hodder Wayland, 1993)

Terry Deary, *The Woeful Second World War* (Scholastic, 1999)

Nigel Kelly and Martyn Whittock, *The Era of the Second World War* (Heinemann, 1993)

Michael Leapman, *Witnesses to War* (Viking-Penguin, 1998)

James Riordan, *The Prisoner* (a children's novel), (Oxford University Press, 1999)

# Glossary

**Allies** Nations joined together against Germany and other 'Axis Powers'; at first mainly Britain, France, Belgium and Holland, later the Soviet Union and the USA.

**Artillery** Heavy guns.

*Blitzkrieg* 'Lightning war' – an intense attack intended to bring about a quick victory.

**Boche** German soldiers. It is French slang meaning 'scoundrels' and was first used in World War I.

**Chaplain** An army vicar or priest.

**Evacuation** Removing people to safety from a place of danger.

**Gangrene** Rotting of the body tissue.

**Jerries** A nickname for Germans.

**Maginot Line** The line of defence built along France's north-eastern frontier, from Switzerland to Luxembourg; completed in 1936 and named after the French foreign minister André Maginot.

**Morphine** A drug used to relieve pain.

**Normandy Landings** In June 1944, Allied troops, mainly British and American, landed on France's Normandy coast with the intention of driving the Nazis back.

**'Operation Dynamo'** The code name for the operation to take soldiers from Dunkirk in hundreds of boats and ships.

**Pontoons** Flat-bottomed boats used for carrying large objects across a river.

**RAF** The British Royal Air Force.

**Refugee** A person trying to escape from danger.

**Reich** (Third Reich) The German state under the rule of Hitler and the Nazi Party (1933–1945).

**Semaphore** A system of sending messages by holding arms or flags in certain positions according to the alphabet.

**SS** (*Schutz-Staffel*) The Nazi special police force.

**Tommies** British soldiers – the name 'Thomas (Tommy) Atkins' was first used for soldiers on official forms in World War I. It became the general name for all British soldiers.

**Transmitter** A radio for broadcasting messages.

**White ensign** A flag used by the Royal Navy.

*Survivors* is a unique collection of fictional stories about young people caught up in real-life conflicts and disasters. Through their eyes we experience the day-to-day hardships and dangers of living through troubled times.

*Another Survivors title from Hodder Wayland*

## THE STAR HOUSES

*Stewart Ross*

*Snipping away the stitching that held on my yellow star, my mother said defiantly, 'Right! That's simple. From now on we won't wear these silly badges. None of us!' When she had finished, she exclaimed, 'There! Now you're just an ordinary Hungarian like everyone else.' If only it had been that simple.*

Bandi Guttmann is a fourteen-year-old Hungarian Jew, living in Budapest in 1944. German forces have occupied the city and life for Bandi and his family is about to become unbearable. Set apart from the rest of the Hungarian community, and denied basic human rights, the family's only weapon is their determination to survive. But in the face of mindless hatred, will the Guttmanns' strength, love and courage be enough to hold them together?

*The Star Houses* is based on the memoirs of Andor Guttmann.

## THE WATER PUPPETS

*Clive Gifford*

*Seven white crosses . . . Seven men dead. Xuan shuddered at the thought. What was the point of such death? Seven soldiers must have died right here on this deserted, lonely road. 'Why?' Xuan wondered to himself.*

The farmers of Noy Thien village have enough of a war on their hands with the seasons, the monsoon and the soil – they have no reason to fight anything else. But this is Vietnam and it's 1967. The country is divided and American troops have moved in. For thirteen-year-old Xuan and his family, their world is about to be turned upside down. Neighbours are fighting each other and no one is certain who the real enemy is. Can life for Xuan's family ever be the same again?

*Another Survivors title from Hodder Wayland*

## BROKEN LIVES

*Neil Tonge*

*All that could be heard in the stillness of that frosty morning was the hum of the machinery and the slap of the ropes, drawing the men to the pithead as if a spider was spinning its web and they were insects caught in its threads . . .*

It's the 1840s in a Victorian mining town and disaster is about to strike. For young John Elliot and his family, life in the shadow of the grinding colliery wheel has always been hard, but there is no alternative for folk like them. The risks are huge and the rewards are few. The Elliots are about to discover the real cost of daring to dig deeper than any worms will ever go . . .

# ORDER FORM

Other titles in the SURVIVORS series:

*All Hodder Children's books are available at your local bookshop or newsagent, or can be ordered direct from the publisher. Just tick the titles you want and fill in the form below. Prices and availability subject to change without notice.*

Hodder Wayland, Cash Sales Department, Bookpoint, 130 Milton Park, Abingdon, OXON, OX14 4TD, UK. If you have a credit card, our call team would be delighted to take your order by telephone. Our direct line is *01235 400414* (lines open 9.00 am–6.00 pm Monday to Saturday, 24 hour message answering service). Alternatively you can send a fax on *01235 400454*.

Or please enclose a cheque or postal order made payable to Bookpoint Ltd to the value of the cover price and allow the following for postage and packing:
UK & BFPO – £1.00 for the first book, 50p for the second book, and 30p for each additional book ordered up to a maximum charge of £3.00.
OVERSEAS & EIRE – £2.00 for the first book, £1.00 for the second book, and 50p for each additional book.

Name ...........................................................................................................................

Address .......................................................................................................................

.......................................................................................................................

.......................................................................................................................

If you would prefer to pay by credit card, please complete:
Please debit my Visa/Access/Diner's Card/American Express (delete as applicable) card no:

| | | | | | | | | | | | | | | | |
|---|---|---|---|---|---|---|---|---|---|---|---|---|---|---|---|

Signature ....................................................................................................................

Expiry Date ................................................................................................................